P9-CFN-263

Put Beginning Readers on the Right Track with ALL ABOARD READING™

The All Aboard Reading series is especially for beginning readers. Written by noted authors and illustrated in full color, these are books that children really and truly *want* to read—books to excite their imagination, tickle their funny bone, expand their interests, and support their feelings. With four different reading levels, All Aboard Reading lets you choose which books are most appropriate for your children and their growing abilities.

Picture Readers—for Ages 3 to 6
Picture Readers have super-simple texts, with many nouns appearing as rebus pictures. At the end of each book are 24 flash cards—on one side is the rebus picture; on the other side is the written-out word.

Level 1—for Preschool through First-Grade Children
Level 1 books have very few lines per page, very large type, easy words, lots of repetition, and pictures with visual "cues" to help children figure out the words on the page.

Level 2—for First-Grade to Third-Grade Children
Level 2 books are printed in slightly smaller type than Level 1 books. The stories are more complex, but there is still lots of repetition in the text, and many pictures. The sentences are quite simple and are broken up into short lines to make reading easier.

Level 3—for Second-Grade through Third-Grade Children
Level 3 books have considerably longer texts, harder words, and more complicated sentences.

All Aboard for happy reading!

For Hadassah Brooks Morgan,
with love —D.H.

To my mother and father
—N.C.

Text copyright © 1995 by Deborah Hautzig. Illustrations copyright © 1995 by Natalie Carabetta. All rights reserved. Adapted from Frances Hodgson Burnett's *The Secret Garden*. Published by Grosset & Dunlap, Inc., a member of Penguin Putnam Books for Young Readers, New York. ALL ABOARD READING is a trademark of The Putnam & Grosset Group. GROSSET & DUNLAP is a trademark of Grosset & Dunlap, Inc. Published simultaneously in Canada. Printed in the U.S.A.

Library of Congress Cataloging-in-Publication Data

Burnett, Frances Hodgson, 1849–1924.
    Frances Hodgson Burnett's The secret garden / adapted by Deborah Hautzig ; illustrated by Natalie Carabetta.
        p.   cm. — (All aboard reading)
    Summary: Ten-year-old Mary comes to live in a lonely house on the Yorkshire moors and discovers an invalid cousin and the mysteries of a locked garden.
        [1. Orphans—Fiction.   2. Gardens—Fiction.   3. Physically handicapped—Fiction.
    4. Yorkshire (England)—Fiction.]   I. Carabetta, Natalie, ill.   II. Burnett, Frances Hodgson, 1849–1924. Secret garden.   III. Title.   IV. Series.
PZ7.B934Fr   1995
[Fic]—dc20   94-26078
                                                                                                      CIP

ISBN 0-448-40736-1   G H I J

ALL
ABOARD
READING™
Level 3
Grades 2-3

The Secret Garden

Adapted from Frances Hodgson Burnett's
The Secret Garden
By Deborah Hautzig
Illustrated by Natalie Carabetta

Grosset & Dunlap • New York

Mary Lennox was born in India. She was a pale, thin, sour little girl. She never laughed. She never even smiled.

Mary hardly ever saw her parents. They were much too busy. So Mary was raised by servants—servants who always had to do what she ordered.

Then, when Mary was ten years old, her life changed forever. A terrible sickness swept through India. All the servants died. Mary's parents died, too. When Mary found out, she wasn't sad. She was angry.

"Who will take care of me?" she said, stamping her foot.

Mary got her answer soon enough. She was put on a ship and sent to England. She was going to live with Archibald Craven—an uncle she had never even met.

When the ship reached England, a servant named Mrs. Medlock hurried Mary into a coach. All during the long ride, the servant talked about Mary's new home.

"It's a gloomy old house with one hundred rooms. Most are shut up, of course," said Mrs. Medlock. "Your uncle's wife died ten years ago. Ever since, he has been strange and sad."

Mary kept quiet.

Mrs. Medlock went on. "He's got a crooked back, did you know? He stays away most of the time. He's traveling now and won't be home for months."

"I don't care," said Mary.

"What a sour little thing you are!" said Mrs. Medlock. "Just like him!"

From then on Mrs. Medlock kept quiet, too.

After crossing miles of bare, wild land, at last they arrived at a huge, dark house. Mrs. Medlock led Mary through a long hallway. There were dark paintings of grim-looking people on the walls. It was so unfriendly and cold!

"This is where you will live," Mrs. Medlock said, opening the door to a gloomy room. "Do NOT wander around the house!" Then she left, closing the door firmly behind her.

Mary had never felt so lost or so lonely in her life.

The next day, Mary woke to see a young, smiling maid. "Good morning!" said the girl. "My name is Martha. Come and eat your breakfast."

"I'm not hungry," Mary said crossly. "Who will dress me?"

Martha was amazed. "Can't you dress yourself?"

"No!" said Mary. "In India my servants dressed me."

"It is time to learn," Martha said. "I will help. Then you can go outside."

It looked cold and wintry from the window. "What would I do outside?" Mary asked.

"What? My little brother Dickon plays outside all day! He makes friends with the animals," Martha told her. "You must go out, too, and see the gardens." Then Martha whispered, "All but one. One garden is locked up."

"Why is it locked?" asked Mary.

"It belonged to your uncle's wife. When she died, he locked the door and buried the key. No one has been inside for ten years."

Ten years! Mary thought. That was as long as she had been alive. She did not say anything to Martha. But she began to feel curious about this locked garden.

Outside, Mary began to wander.

Everything was bare and gray, except
for a robin with a bright red breast. There
were lawns and orchards and gardens
with stone walls and doors. But the
doors were wide open. Where was the
special garden?

Mary saw an old man digging.
"Who are you?" she demanded.
"I'm Ben—the gardener," he growled.

Just then the little robin landed right on his foot. Ben's face lit up. "That's my robin!" he said. "He's lonely. So he made friends with me."

Mary had no friends at all. She stared at the pretty bird. "Will you be my friend?" she whispered to it.

The robin chirped happily, and Mary couldn't help herself. She smiled!

Suddenly the robin flew away—over a high wall covered with ivy. "Where did he go?" cried Mary. "Is that the garden that was locked?"

Instantly Ben was grumpy again. "Stop asking so many questions," he said, and stomped off.

That was when Mary made up her mind to find the hidden garden...all by herself.

The next day and every day after that, Mary went looking for a door in the ivy-covered wall. "I won't give up till I find it," she promised herself.

Before she knew it, Mary was
spending whole days outside. Martha
even taught her to skip rope.

All the fresh air was making Mary
very hungry. She was eating more than
she ever had. Soon pale, thin Mary
started looking pretty and rosy!

One day Mary heard a friendly "chirp-chirp" behind her. It was the robin. He was following her!

"You remember me!" cried Mary happily.

The robin hopped and fluttered and finally settled near the wall. Suddenly Mary saw a gleam in the dirt. She touched it and gasped. It was a key. It had to be the key to the secret garden!

"You helped me find the key," Mary
said to the robin. "Can you help me
find the door?"

As the robin flew to the top of the
stone wall, a strong wind came up. It
blew the ivy away, and there it
was—a door!

Mary was so excited that her hand shook as she turned the key in the keyhole.

The door opened, and Mary
slipped inside. She was in the secret
garden! The garden was strange and
magical. There were little stone benches
and fountains and archways. Gray
vines hung from all the leafless trees.
It was wild and untidy and beautiful.

"I want to make this garden come alive again," Mary whispered. "And it will be my secret. My wonderful secret garden!"

That night Mary could hardly sleep for imagining how she would save the garden. By morning she knew just what to do.

"Martha," she said, "I wish I had a shovel and some seeds. I want to make things grow." Of course, she did not say where.

Martha smiled. "My brother Dickon can help. I will ask him."

"Oh, thank you, Martha!" cried Mary happily. "You are as nice as the robin." Now Mary had two friends!

On the next sunny day Mary found
a boy sitting under a tree, playing
a wooden pipe. Watching him were a
fox, a lamb, a rabbit, and a crow.

"I'm Dickon," said the boy. "You
must be Mary. I have your tools and
seeds. I will even help you plant them.
Where is your garden?"

Mary looked at Dickon. "Can you
keep a secret?" she asked softly.

"Oh my, yes. That's why animals
trust me," he said.

"I've stolen a garden," Mary
whispered. "I'll show you."

Mary led Dickon through the hidden door. "It's like a dream," he said softly. He touched the trees and the vines and the bushes. "These are still alive. They just need someone to care for them."

"They have us!" said Mary.

After that, Mary and Dickon worked in the garden every day. And every day they had picnics under the archways. Mary had never been so busy or so happy.

Late one night, Mary woke up. Rain was beating on her window. But there was another noise, too. It sounded like someone crying.

In the morning she asked Martha what it was. "Only the wind," Martha said quickly.

But Mary was not so sure.

The next night the sound was louder.
"That's not the wind," Mary said to
herself. "Someone is crying." She got
out of bed and tiptoed through the long,
dark halls. The crying sounded closer
and closer.

She saw a glimmer of light under a door and pushed it open. There, in a big carved bed, was a boy!

"Who...who are you? Are you a ghost?" he asked.

"No," said Mary. "I am Mary Lennox. I live here. Mr. Craven is my uncle. Who are you?"

"I am Colin Craven," said the boy. "Mr. Craven is my father."

"Your father!" gasped Mary. "Nobody told me he had a son!"

"I am sick and hate for anyone to see me. If I live, I will have a crooked back. But I won't live. Everyone says so." An angry shadow passed across his face. "My mother died when I was born. Now my father hates to be with me. I remind him of losing her."

"He hates her garden, too," said Mary. Then she wished she hadn't.

"What garden?" asked Colin.

"The garden that was locked ten years ago," said Mary nervously.

"Why was it locked?" asked Colin eagerly. "What is it like now?"

Poor Colin, thought Mary. He is just like I was when I came here, with nothing to do and no one to care for.

"Can you keep a secret?" whispered Mary.

"Yes!" said Colin. "Yes!"

So Mary told Colin all about the secret garden. And about Dickon and his animals.

"I want to see this garden," Colin said.

"Can you go outside?" asked Mary.

"I can do anything I want. Everyone has to please me," said Colin sharply. "I have a wheelchair. You and Dickon will push me."

Mary laughed. Colin was spoiled, just like she had been.

So Colin began to go out every morning with Mary and Dickon. Nobody knew where they went. Like a young prince, he ordered the servants to keep away from them.

The secret garden was their private kingdom. Spring was coming. The children watched as the garden turned into a rainbow of color.

And slowly, very slowly, Colin began to change, too. He looked stronger every day, and happier.

One afternoon the children were
having so much fun they made more
noise than usual. Suddenly Colin saw a
face looking over the garden wall. It was
Ben, on a ladder. "Are you Mr. Craven's
son, the poor cripple?" he asked.

"I'm NOT a cripple!" cried Colin.
"There is nothing wrong with me at all."

Then Colin gripped the arms of his wheelchair—and stood up!

Mary and Dickon stared at Colin, amazed. He had never stood before.

"Everyone said I was sick, so I believed it, too," Colin said. "But you and Dickon showed me I could live and be well. You believed in me. And you were right!"

"It's the garden," said Mary.

"Yes," said Dickon. "The garden is magic."

Colin turned to Ben. "Please remember," he said, "this garden is a secret. And you cannot tell ANYBODY that I am well. I want to surprise my father when he comes home."

"I won't say a word," said Ben.

"Oh, I hope he comes soon," said Colin.

And then, a few weeks later, Mr. Craven finally did come home. Usually he went right to his room and saw no one. But this time was different. Something made him walk as quickly as he could to the locked garden.

When he reached it, he stopped, amazed. He heard sounds. The sounds of children laughing and running.

Then all at once, the garden door burst open. A tall, handsome boy ran right into Mr. Craven.

"Who…who are you?" Mr. Craven gasped.

"Father, I am Colin," said the boy. "I am well. I am well!"

Mr. Craven held his son close.
"I thought you would die," he said.
"Mary and Dickon and the
garden made me well," said Colin.
"The garden?" said Mr. Craven.

Colin said, "We cared for it and loved it and made it come alive. And Mary and I came alive with it. It was like magic, Father. Like magic!"

Now the secret garden wasn't a secret anymore. But its magic would be with them forever.